GHOST TOWER

ReadZone Books Limited
www.ReadZoneBooks.com

© in this edition 2017 ReadZone Books Limited

This print edition published in cooperation with Fiction Express, who first published this title in weekly instalments as an interactive e-book.

FICTION EXPRESS

Fiction Express
Boolino Limited
First Floor Office, 2 College Street,
Ludlow, Shropshire SY8 1AN
www.fictionexpress.co.uk

Find out more about Fiction Express on pages 94–95.

Design: Laura Harrison & Keith Williams
Cover Image: Bigstock

© in the text 2016 Andrew G Taylor
The moral right of the author has been asserted.

ISBN 978-1-78322-605-4

Printed in Malta by Melita Press

GHOST TOWER

ANDREW G TAYLOR

What do other readers think?

Here are some comments left on the Fiction Express blog about this book:

"This chapter was awesome. I love this book and cannot wait until the next chapter comes out."
Erina

"This book is really exciting. I can't wait to see what happens in the next chapter. I hope there are lots more books to come like Ghost Tower soon."
Lizzie

"[I] loved the book. I'm really sad it's ended. However I loved all the excitement. I cannot wait to read another book from you."
Seth

"Your book is awesome and scary."
Zander, Justin and Alex

"This has been exhilarating all the way through. I could not stop reading this. In my opinion you are the best writer, thanks for the great chapters."
Alexander

Contents

Chapter 1

The Shang Tower

Never take the underpass after dark. That had been drummed into Leanne ever since she'd been walking to school by herself. She peered into the darkness beneath the main road that snaked through the grim Larkrise Estate. She had no choice – she was already late!

She sprinted into the tunnel. The overhead lights flickered. *Just keep moving*, she told herself, shifting the backpack on her shoulder. Her dad's bolt cutters inside clinked against the heavy metal torch.

She ran up the ramp on the far side and hurried to the bus stop, where Hamid was waiting.

"What kept you?" he demanded, looking around nervously.

"Dad went to bed late," she said, pushing her long flame-red hair behind her ears as she caught her breath. "Let's get going."

Leanne led the way across a deserted playground and through a line of trees. And then they saw it rising menacingly into the ink-black sky.

"The Shang Tower," whispered Leanne, casting her eyes up the unlit floors of the apartment block. Although she knew the building was deserted, she had the strangest feeling someone was watching them from up there. A shiver went through her.

"Hard to believe it's going to be blown up at dawn," said Hamid. "Think it's safe?"

"Don't worry," she said as they reached the chain-link fence around the demolition site. "Dad says they don't put the blasting charges in until the last minute. For tonight we have the place all to ourselves."

Hamid glanced nervously at the 'SECURITY PATROLS: KEEP OUT' sign as Leanne set to work snipping an opening in the fence. Hamid held it open so she could slip through, then followed close behind.

They ran towards the tower. The ground was uneven, churned up by the diggers that had been busy clearing this part of the Larkrise Estate over the last six months. *The Shang's all that's left of the old slums*, thought Leanne as she ran between the shadows. *And tomorrow at dawn even that will be dust.*

She reached the main doors to the tower first. There was a chain looped between the handles, fastened by a heavy padlock. But it was no match for the bolt cutters....

As the door slammed shut behind them, Leanne shone her torch around. The entrance hall was covered in rubbish and debris left behind when the building had been cleared. There was a rank smell in the air, but it was the graffiti that caused them both to catch their breath.

Across one wall someone had spray-painted *EVIL LIVES HERE* in red lettering as tall as a man. Clearly one of the Larkrise graffiti artists had a dark sense of humour…. But it gave Leanne the same chill she'd felt earlier.

"Tell me again why we're doing this?" Hamid asked.

It would be about the fiftieth time she'd told him the story, but Leanne guessed her friend needed reassurance.

"There's treasure hidden on the top floor," she said. "My granddad told me about an antiques collector who lived up there. He hid his valuables in the walls…. Under the floorboards…. He was terrified of being robbed. Then one day he died suddenly. His treasure was never found."

"Perhaps it wasn't there."

"Perhaps no one was actually *looking* for it! C'mon, Hamid!" said Leanne. "If we don't find anything, we'll just go home. But wouldn't you hate for all that stuff to be blown up with the tower? Imagine how much it could be worth!"

Hamid frowned. "How much?"

"Enough to get our families off the Larkrise, for a start."

Hamid's expression softened at that, and Leanne knew she had him once again. He hated living on the estate even more than she did.

"So what are we waiting for?" he said finally. Leanne grinned and led the way towards the far side of the lobby.

"This should lead to the stairwell," she said, pushing open a green door, with a screech of unoiled hinges. She was relieved to see concrete stairs leading up in the torch beam.

They climbed in silence for a while, aware of every creak and groan from the empty building. A moaning wind whistled through the broken window panes.

"What was that?" demanded Hamid. Leanne angled the torch towards a scuttling sound above them. Shadows danced in the beam.

"Probably just a rat," she said.

"That's it! I'm out of here," said Hamid.

Leanne turned. "Wait!" she said, grabbing his arm. There was something moving in the darkness below them. All she could see in the torchlight was its shadow. It seemed to grow in size as it approached, moving up the walls. Long shadowy fingers stretched out towards them…. "Up!" cried Leanne, pulling Hamid along with her now. But as they turned, the beam of her torch illuminated a second shadow on the landing above them. It was leaning down over the railing… fingers extending…. A screeching sound filled the air….

Chapter 2

The Shades

Leanne yanked open the door labelled *Seventh Floor* and pushed Hamid through. They pulled it closed again as something slammed against the other side, screeching wildly. The force of the blow almost knocked Leanne off her feet. She braced as the door was hit again.

"What *are* those things?" whispered Hamid.

Leanne shone the torch around, picking up a litter-strewn corridor. Her mind was racing. All thoughts of getting to the top floor forgotten – now all she wanted to do was get out of the tower.

"Look!" said Hamid, breaking her train of thought. He nodded at a door at the far end of the corridor. It was slightly ajar, allowing a thin, yellowish light to escape from inside.

The stairwell door rocked again. This time the force was enough to tear one of the hinges free. Leanne raised her torch and the beam picked up a shadow finger creeping through the crack towards them.

"Nothing casts a shadow like that!" said Hamid as they backed away.

"I don't think anything is *casting* the shadow!" Leanne gasped. "The shadow's all there is." At that moment, the stairwell door hinges gave way completely.

Leanne and Hamid sprinted down the corridor, leaping over discarded packing boxes and other, nastier, things as they went. The screeching of the shadow monsters sounded terrifyingly close behind them, but Leanne didn't look back. As they reached the open door, a grey-haired man appeared as if he had been waiting for them. They dashed into the flat and he slammed the door shut after them, throwing a deadbolt to hold it in place.

Leanne pressed herself to the wall, staring at the closed door... expecting the shadows to start pounding it down.... But there was only the faint sound of a frustrated screech from the other side.

"It's okay," said the man quietly as he removed a cloth from his tweed jacket and started cleaning his wire-framed glasses with it. With his smart appearance and shock of white hair, he had the look of a professor. "That should keep the Shades out for a while."

Hamid, was crouching on the carpeted floor, breathing heavily. "Shades?"

"Those shadow creatures that chased you up here," said the man, matter-of-factly, stepping past Hamid through a door that led to a tiny lounge. "Come on. We haven't much time."

Hamid looked at Leanne and hissed, "Who *is* this guy? He gives me the creeps!"

She grabbed his hand and pulled him to his feet. "I'd rather be in here with *him* than out there with... well, who knows what, wouldn't you?"

Leanne led the way into the lounge. In contrast to the rest of the tower, it was clean and well-kept. Light was provided by dozens of candles set around the room. Their flickering glow illuminated walls covered with framed photographs, some colour, some black and white. There were hundreds of them.

"They're photos of the tower," Leanne said. Many were images of the building itself – empty rooms, corridors, stairs – but some showed people. Men, women, children, families, workers, gangs of kids…. But these weren't the type of happy shots people posted to Facebook. Every person stared from their photo with a blank expression. The appearance unsettled her. "Did you take them?"

"Some of them," said the man, who was busying himself with a worn leather satchel at a table in the centre of the room. "Some I collected over the years."

"Who are they?"

"Former residents of the tower," he said, then

shook his head and muttered, "or something like that."

Hamid came to Leanne's side. "How come you're here?"

The old man smiled for the first time. "I could ask the same of you two."

Leanne and Hamid exchanged a sheepish look. She began, "We're... uh–"

"Let me guess," the man interrupted, "looking for hidden treasure. You wouldn't believe the number of people who have been lured in over the years by that old tale." His smile turned into something darker, almost a grimace. "The tower has a way of trapping people. Looks as if it's found its two last victims."

Hamid pressed his face close to Leanne's ear and whispered, "This guy's nuts!"

"No, perfectly sane," said the man. He stepped forward and offered a bony hand for Leanne to shake. "Solomon Burke," he continued, as she took his hand. "But you can call me Sol. I'm the last remaining resident of the Shang Tower. I've lived here since it was built, more than sixty years ago. Over time, I came to realize something…."

Sol paused for effect, staring down at them, blue eyes sparking with intensity in the candlelight.

"Something evil lives inside this tower," he said. "Something that has claimed the lives of dozens of people over the years. Maybe hundreds. Their souls are trapped here. Two of them tried to attack you in the corridor just now."

Leanne shook her head slowly. "You're saying those things out there… are ghosts?"

Hamid tugged on her arm and hissed, "*We have to get out of here!*"

"Hungry ghosts," continued Sol, turning back to the table. "They died here and now they serve the evil that dwells in this place."

"What *is* this evil?" asked Leanne, intrigued.

"I'm not sure exactly," said the old man, "but I know it was brought here by an antiques collector."

"The one who lived here in the tower?" asked Leanne, remembering her grandfather's story.

"Yes," said Sol. "He discovered a fascinating artefact on an archaeological dig many years ago in China. It contained a force of great power. The Collector brought it home, and it's power has grown in this place. But the evil is trapped here in the tower, as are those whose lives it has claimed." He looked back at Leanne and Hamid sharply. "But don't take my word for it… ask them."

He waved an arm expansively around the rows of photographs. Leanne's gaze followed the gesture, noting the faces seemed to move in the candlelight.

Wait… they *were* moving!

"Help us!" a woman cried from a black and white picture. She was holding a baby in her arms.

"Set us free!" called two little girls, sitting side by side in another photograph.

"Don't turn your back on us!" demanded a man with wild, accusing eyes.

"Save us from this evil!" another begged.

Soon the room was filled with a cacophony of voices calling from Sol's library of photos. As Leanne moved to cover her ears, the old man made a cutting motion with his hand. The photographs fell silent immediately, although the mouths of the people still moved wordlessly.

WHAM

The front door of the flat was hit hard by the Shades. Sol moved into action, grabbing three photographs from the walls and laying them out in a triangle on the tabletop.

"The door won't hold much longer," he said. "We have to leave now."

"Leave?" demanded Leanne. "We can't go out there!"

Sol shook his head and pointed to the photographs on the table. "Through these. Notice anything about them?"

Leanne and Hamid stepped forward and looked down at the photographs. One showed a family portrait, a mother, father and twin boys aged about eight. Another showed a man staring intently out of the picture at them. The third showed an empty room filled with antiques that made Leanne think immediately of the story of the Collector.

"There's a shadow in them all," said Hamid. Then Leanne saw it too – a dark blur behind the family… and around the man… and in the empty room.

"Well spotted," said Sol. "A trace of the evil in the past."

The Shades slammed against the door again. Sol fished inside his satchel and removed a brass key. As he waved it over the pictures, they began to take on more definition and depth, like a 3D image. They seemed to grow beyond the frame. "The portals are opening!" explained Sol.

There was a crash as the front door gave way. Suddenly the room was a maelstrom of swirling air, that extinguished half the candles. In the remaining light, Leanne could see the Shades crawling slowly across the floor towards them

"What do we have to do?" she demanded.

"I'm beginning to think you were sent here tonight for a reason!" Sol yelled over the sound of the screeching. "There's three pictures…. Three of us…. Three pieces of a puzzle to solve… and we just might destroy the evil in this place forever!" He handed the key to Leanne. "You need to choose where we start!"

More of the candles went out. The room was almost in total darkness now and the Shades were moving in….

The Collector, thought Leanne as she reached for Hamid's hand and pulled him towards the picture of the antique-filled room. As she moved forward, Solomon's bony fingers closed on her shoulder. The picture expanded before them, filling Leanne's vision as she held out the key. There was a rush of air… a powerful sensation of being pushed across an invisible barrier….

And then they were in the picture.

Leanne released Hamid's hand and looked around the room, which was similar to Sol's in layout but completely different in appearance. There was plush carpet underfoot and the space was crammed with antiques, most of them Oriental in appearance: porcelain dragons, plates with blue-tinted pictures and ornate tapestries with Chinese writing. Leanne turned, expecting to see Sol's simple apartment behind them… but the portal had closed.

"Look at all this stuff!" Hamid said in a hushed tone, picking up a carved ivory box from a nearby table. "This must be the Collector's apart–"

"Don't touch anything!" snapped Sol with unexpected urgency, but it was too late!

As Hamid flipped open the lid, a puff of black smoke escaped from the box and enveloped him. He staggered back, knees buckling. Leanne caught him before he hit the floor, gently laying him down.

"Hamid, wake up!" cried Leanne, trying to shake him awake. Her friend was out cold. She looked at Sol. "What's wrong with him?"

"He's breathing, but unconscious." Sol gave her a hard look. "The Tower is a place of many secrets and dangers. We need to be more cautious."

The sound of approaching footsteps made them both look round in alarm.

"The Collector!" whispered Leanne.

"We need to get out, Leanne," urged Sol. "It would be a bad idea for all three of us to be found here."

"What about Hamid?" she asked.

Sol shook his head. "The important thing is for us to get away – our mission is vital. We'll have to leave him behind." Then, seeing the concern in Leanne's eyes, he added, "For now at least."

The footsteps were approaching the room.

Leanne looked round desperately, weighing up her possible options....

Chapter 3

"Trust No one"

The footsteps grew steadily louder. Leanne rose to her feet, determined to stand and face whoever… or whatever… was approaching.

"What are you doing?" demanded Sol, grabbing her arm. "We have to get out of here, NOW!"

But it was too late. An elderly Chinese woman appeared amidst the antiques. She was short, barely reaching Leanne's shoulder, and dressed in a beautifully crafted blue robe with gold embroidery.

Surely she *could not be the Collector?*

"Who are *you*?" the woman gasped. She reached for a battered umbrella from a wooden stand and brandished it. "Back thieves!"

"We're not thieves," protested Leanne. "We're…we're travellers from the future. I know that sounds crazy…" she tailed off.

To her surprise the woman lowered her makeshift weapon. "What have you come for?" she asked, piercing Leanne with her dark eyes.

Leanne took a breath, wondering what to say next. "We're trying to stop the evil that's taken hold of this tower," she said, matter-of-factly.

"I see," mumbled the woman, nodding as if she understood completely. "Come with me." She beckoned to Leanne.

"But my friend," said Leanne urgently, gesturing at Hamid who lay unconscious on the floor, the ivory box still clutched in his hand. "He opened that box and… well, it knocked him out somehow."

"Oh, it's just a herbal mix I made, to catch thieves in the act. He'll recover any moment." Even as she said this, Hamid began to open his eyes.

"What happened?" he said, looking round wildly.

"You're ok," Leanne soothed, placing a hand on his shoulder. "But don't touch anything else," she warned.

"Come," said the woman, and Leanne followed her through the rows of antiques while Sol helped Hamid to his feet.

"Sorry we frightened you," Leanne began.

The woman dismissed Leanne's concern with a graceful wave of her hand. Her beautiful silk robe rippled with the movement, reminding Leanne of waves on a beach. "My name is Jing Shi," she said, her voice barely a cracked whisper. "I too am doing what I can to fight against the Collector and his evil."

"You know about the Collector?" Leanne asked.

"Yes, child," sighed the lady, "though I do not know his real identity… nobody does." She moved further away, stopping at a table adorned with oriental tapestries. Dragons and spirits intricately woven in gold glared out at them.

Checking to make sure that Sol and Hamid could not hear her, she continued, "The Collector stole an item of great power from my homeland – an urn that imprisons demons from the earliest days of China. The Collector drew immense power from these demons. They extended his life, gave him the ability to cross time and control men's minds."

The woman drew back one of the tapestries, revealing a row of jade bottles.

"Over the years the urn decayed and the demons escaped. One of them is a mighty but mystical Dragon. I believe it is living in the basement of the tower, though I have not dared to venture there. I am too old and weak to take on such a battle."

Jing Shi looked hard at Leanne, her dark eyes shining fiercely. "You, child, must fight this Dragon! Defeat it and you will gain one part of a powerful weapon to end the evil once and for all." She held up a warning finger. "But beware. The power of the demons corrupts all who come into contact with them. Trust no one!"

She handed Leanne one of the jade bottles.

It felt warm in her hand and glowed brightly as she held it.

"Use this against the Dragon," said the old woman before cupping Leanne's hands in her own, the bottle clenched tightly between them. "Trust your own instincts and make your own decisions. Have faith in yourself – I believe you have the courage to save us all."

Jing Shi drew back immediately as Sol appeared, closely followed by a groggy-looking Hamid. Leanne slipped the jade bottle into her pocket.

"There's a Shade," Hamid said urgently. "It's found us!"

He pointed to the other side of the room where a shadow was growing, elongated fingers probing between the rows of furniture.

Jing Shi removed something from her robes and threw it at the floor. There was a blinding flash and the Shade recoiled, as if stung by the light.

"Run!" she ordered. "I will deal with the darkness."

Leanne hesitated, but Sol grabbed her arm, pulling her away after Hamid. They flew through the apartment as there was a second explosive flash behind them and a high-pitched squealing sound.

Racing down the twisting corridors outside, they eventually found themselves in an open area… a balcony bathed in unexpected sunlight. They paused for breath.

"Will Jing Shi be okay?" Leanne asked.

Sol smiled. "I have a feeling she knows what she's doing. She always was a formidable woman!"

"You know her?" Leanne asked, surprised.

"Uh, well," mumbled Sol, "not really… I remember her a bit from when I was a boy. And of course I have her picture."

Leanne remembered the strange picture gallery on the walls of Sol's flat and shivered slightly.

"Look at all this, Leanne," said Hamid distracting her. She joined him, gazing round at their new surroundings in wonder. The sun was high in the sky and there was the feeling of a cold and clear winter's day. The balcony was on the twentieth floor of the tower, overlooking rows of terraced houses which had been replaced by modern apartments and flyovers in their time.

"I'd say we've travelled back over fifty years," said Sol, answering the question that was in Leanne's mind.

"It's all so different," said Hamid as they turned to look back down the corridor they'd come from. The apartment doors looked freshly painted and there was no litter, no trace of graffiti anywhere. "Maybe we should just stay here," he joked, nudging Leanne.

"Don't be fooled," Sol said grimly. "The evil has already begun to take hold. It's vital we stop it before the tower is destroyed! Which reminds me…." He removed an object from his tweed jacket – a silver pocket watch. "This watch shows us the time back home," he explained. "So we can keep on track."

"It's almost midnight," said Leanne.

"Six hours until dawn," Sol confirmed. "If we let the tower be demolished the evil will be set free forever. I fear it will spread far and wide."

"This is getting ridiculous," huffed Hamid. "We're trapped in this tower, although we've managed to travel through time and now we're expected to battle some mysterious 'evil'! I should never have listened to you, Leanne – I could be fast asleep at home right now."

"If you were," said Sol, turning to glare at the boy. "Then you'd be in grave danger, just as your friends… your family… everyone back home is. If the evil is released from the tower, no one will be safe. The future of the whole human race will be changed forever!"

"And what are *we* supposed to do about that?" cried Hamid. "We're just two kids… and an old man who's never even *tried* fighting this evil before! All you seem to do is hide or run away from it."

"Stop arguing," snapped Leanne. "We're here now and we have a job to do. According to Jing

Shi there's a Dragon demon living in the basement! If we destroy it, we'll be one step closer to ending all this and getting back home."

Before Hamid and Sol could question her, Leanne stomped off towards the nearest lift entrance.

Hamid appeared at her side. "This must be a bad dream, a really bad dream," he mumbled to himself as they stepped into the lift, followed by Sol. "I'm going to pinch myself and wake up any minute now."

Leanne reached out and pinched his arm. He gave a yelp of pain.

"Did you wake up?" she asked.

"No."

"Then let's get on with this!"

Chapter 4

Eyes of the Dragon

As the lift descended with surprising speed, Hamid flashed Leanne a worried look. "You were kidding about the dragon, right? I mean, whoever heard of a–"

"I don't know," Leanne interrupted. "But I guess we're about to find out."

The lift juddered to a halt and the doors slid open onto darkness. Sol leaned close to Leanne and whispered, "Be cautious. I've a feeling we're not alone down here."

She nodded, sensing it as well. Somewhere in the darkness of the basement a dim light was flickering and she heard muffled voices piercing the gloom.

Sol led the way out of the lift, Leanne following close behind. Her eyes adjusted to the darkness quickly, making out thick concrete pillars holding up the foundations of the tower. It made her think of the explosives that would be strapped to these very pillars in her own time… ready to detonate at dawn, unleashing the evil on the world.

That's not going to happen, she told herself.

They moved between the pillars towards the orange glow at the far side of the basement. As they closed in, she made out the shapes of eight men silhouetted against the light. They were standing before a giant metal furnace. The door was open wide, revealing a raging fire within.

Taking cover behind a pillar, Leanne watched the men moving in the intense light and heat of the fire. They were dressed identically in jeans and black leather jackets with the word *Dragons* scrawled crudely on the back. Their hair was slicked down against their skulls, reminding Leanne of black and white pictures she'd seen of motorcycle gangs in the fifties.

Suddenly a low rumble emanated from the depths of the furnace. Leanne felt it vibrating through her bones. In the fire she saw a pair of blazing red eyes appear.

The Dragon!

"Hail the Dragon Master," cried one of the men as they all sank to their knees and bowed before the fire.

"THE COLLECTOR HAS WARNED ME OF STRANGERS FROM ANOTHER TIME," boomed a voice that seemed to belong to the Dragon. "BRING THEM TO ME."

"Of course, master," said one of the men. "We will search for them at once."

"NO NEED," The Dragon hissed. "THEY ARE HERE! IN THE SHADOWS!"

As the gang members turned, the fire flared casting light into every corner. Exposed, Leanne started to flee, but the men were fast and knew the basement well. They surrounded them, grabbing Sol and Hamid roughly. The tallest man pulled Leanne's arms behind her back.

"Let me go!" she protested, struggling against his grip. The man ignored her, dragging her towards the heat of the furnace. At that moment, the huge, scaly body of the Dragon, sleek and trailing fire, burst from the flames. The man pushed Leanne to her knees, keeping a hand on her shoulder as he bowed low again. Hamid knelt to the right of her, his face etched with terror.

Leanne turned to the Dragon, staring into its eyes as she slid her hand inside her pocket, feeling the warmth of the small jade bottle within. The Dragon's face resembled the giant paper dragons she had seen in the Chinese New Year parade. But its manic red eyes were full of malice. They burned into her, studying her with apparent interest.

"WHAT IS YOUR NAME GIRL?" it asked.

"I'm Leanne Ross," she said with as much confidence as she could muster. "Nice to meet you."

"THE COLLECTOR FEARS YOU… I CAN'T IMAGINE WHY!"

"Perhaps because he knows I'm going to defeat you," Leanne countered.

"I'D LIKE TO SEE YOU TRY!" said the Dragon, its fiery tongue flicking between its teeth.

"Be careful what you wish for," said Leanne, pulling the jade bottle from her pocket.

The Dragon's eyes widened as she tossed it into the monster's jaws. There was a shattering sound, followed by a green flash and a blast that lifted Leanne clean off her feet and threw her against the wall. The Dragon writhed in pain, its fire turning into green crystal… and then it shattered, casting fragments of jade across the floor.

Leanne staggered to her feet, seeing the gang members unconscious on the floor around her. "Hamid? Sol?" she cried.

"Over here," said Hamid, supporting Sol as they limped towards her. "That was amazing!"

"Thanks," she grinned looking round at the remains of the Dragon. She saw something glowing amongst them. Reaching down, she picked up a piece of polished grey stone half the size of her palm. It looked like a third of a circle, smooth and perfectly formed in her hand. Sol approached and looked down at the object.

"The first piece of the power amulet of Shang!" he cried.

"What's that?" asked Hamid.

"Well," said Sol, a smile lighting his eyes, "We can use the amulet, to drive the demons back into the urn." Then the smile faded. "Of course we'll need to find the other two pieces first!"

"Well we've made a start," said Leanne, holding out the object to him, but Sol leaped back.

"No!" he said with unexpected force. "Don't give it to me!" Then, in a softer tone, he continued. "You defeated the Dragon, Leanne. It's your prize, not mine."

Nodding, Leanne slipped the stone into her pocket, suddenly aware of a movement to her left. A Shade was closing in on one of the gang members. Suddenly the man opened his eyes and let out a scream as the Shade moved in.

"We've got to help him," Leanne cried as she looked on, horrified. Then something else caught her eye. Another Shade was heading towards her fallen backpack! She watched helplessly as the long shadow fingers reached inside and withdrew the portal key. With a wave of its arm, the Shade cast a shimmering portal against the wall and started towards it.

"We mustn't lose that key!" cried Sol. "It's our only way home!"

Chapter 5

Disaster!

"No!" cried Leanne as Sol leaped after the fleeing Shade. There was a flash of light and he let out a cry of anguish as the portal snapped shut behind him. Sol, the Shade and the key were gone!

"Watch out!" shouted Hamid, pointing to the other side of the basement. The gang members had all come round and fled from the Shade, making for the exit. Now the monster was turning its attention to Hamid and Leanne. Blocking their path, it floated across the basement, shadowy fingers outstretched.

Hamid ran to the smouldering remains of the Dragon's furnace. "Jing Shi used bright light to fight that Shade!" he cried, pulling two burning pieces of wood from the flames. "Maybe we can do the same with fire."

As the Shade pounced, Leanne grabbed one of the flaming torches and thrust it towards the creature's grasping hands. The Shade recoiled with a high-pitched squeal. Hamid joined her, slashing the air with his torch. The Shade shrank away from the arc of fire.

"Let's get out of here!" exclaimed Leanne and they started backing towards the stairs, grabbing her backpack on the way. Snarling now, their attacker followed at some distance. As Leanne put her foot on the first step, she threw the torch hard at the Shade. "Run!"

They took the stairs two at a time, slamming the door shut behind them when they reached the top. Looking around, Leanne realized they were standing in the lobby of the Shang Tower. The walls were bright, clean and graffiti-free. A couple walking in the direction of the lifts gave them a puzzled glance, shocked no doubt at their soot-smeared clothes.

"We've lost Sol *and* the portal key!" said Hamid. "Does this mean we're stuck in the 1950s? My mum and dad aren't even born yet!"

Hearing the desperation in his voice, Leanne placed a reassuring hand on his arm. "I think I know someone who can help. Come on!"

They raced back up the tower. Jing Shi answered her apartment door on the second knock.

"I knew I was right to have faith in you," she said with a smile, as if unsurprised to see Leanne. Then she glanced at Hamid. "But where is your other companion?"

Hurrying into the apartment, Leanne explained what had happened to Sol and the portal key. With a grim expression, Jing Shi led them to a twelve-sided table with the animals of the Chinese zodiac carved into its surface. Leanne stared at them as she tried to identify each animal.

Jing Shi placed an ornate metal bowl in the centre of the table, clear water glistening inside.

She motioned them forward as she cast a handful of sweet-smelling powder across the surface of the liquid.

"These waters show many things," she said softly. "The past. The future. Distant places."

"Sol," whispered Leanne, leaning in closer. Sure enough, an image was starting to form in the water.

She saw the flickering shape of the Shade, the key clutched in its hand. This faded and was quickly replaced with Sol's face. Leanne stifled a cry as she saw that he was pinned to the ground by a hairy brown leg. A dark shape descended towards him…. Two gleaming white fangs and a dozen eyes blocked Sol from view….

"What *is* that?" asked Hamid, struggling to keep his voice calm as the image faded.

"It seems your friend has found the next demon you must face – the Spider!" Jing Shi replied. "Beware, it is more powerful than the Dragon! It controls a twisted version of the Shang Tower, full of tricks and traps for the unwary."

"What sort of twisted version?" asked Leanne.

"The Spider's realm is another dimension, somewhere between our reality and the world of darkness," Jing Shi explained, her eyes shining with concern. "If I send you, there will be no coming back until you have defeated the demon."

The words of the Chinese woman sent a spear of dread through Leanne's heart, but she nodded resolutely. "Send me. I'll take the risk alone."

"No way," cried Hamid.

"It's going to be really dangerous," said Leanne.

"I know, but we need to stick together. Send both of us," demanded Hamid, turning to Jing Shi. "Uh… please," he added as the elderly lady glared at him sternly.

"Are you sure you are both up to the task," she asked, turning her gaze on Leanne.

She remembered Jing Shi's former words about trusting no one. "Yes," she replied. "I trust Hamid with my life."

"We're in this together to the end," Hamid added. "Which might be pretty soon if we can't beat this Spider."

Without another word, Jing Shi walked to the centre of the room and drew a circle on the floorboards with white chalk. She motioned for Leanne and Hamid to stand inside.

"I cannot give you a weapon against this demon," she said as they took their positions. "But I have heard a rumour…" she sighed. "The answer is in the demon's legs."

"What does that mean?" asked Leanne.

"Alas, that is all I can tell you," Jing Shi said sadly. "I pray we shall meet again!"

With that, Jing Shi threw a glass bottle at their feet. As it shattered, a brilliant wall of light enveloped them. Hamid grabbed Leanne's hand. The floor dropped from under their feet. A cry caught in Leanne's throat at the sensation of falling… fast!

Chapter 6

The Spider's Web

Leanne's feet hit ground with a bone-shaking impact, and both she and Hamid rolled forward, landing in a heap.

With a groan, Leanne pressed her hand to a cold stone floor and pushed herself into a sitting position. In the semi-darkness she could make out a large circular room. It reminded her of a fairytale dungeon. High above them a circular opening in the ceiling let in a little light.

"This doesn't look anything like the Shang Tower!" whispered Hamid.

"I guess that means we're in the realm of the Spider," said Leanne, shuddering involuntarily.

A scuttling noise echoed from above as a shadowy bulk crossed the opening, momentarily blocking out all the light.

"This might be a very bad time to admit it," Hamid whispered in the darkness. "But I'm arachnophobic."

"I'm not keen on spiders myself," admitted Leanne, turning her attention to the demon as it crawled down the wall and into the room. Its body was bloated and covered in brown and orange hair. Eight armoured legs twitched on either side of its body. The Spider's head bore the massive fangs of a tarantula, topped by a dozen unblinking eyes. It was staring down directly at her with a deadly cunning.

"FOOLISH CHILDREN," the Spider's voice drifted down. Its tone was silky soft, with a deadly edge of menace. "FEW MORTALS ENTER THIS DUNGEON OF THEIR OWN FREE WILL. EVEN FEWER LEAVE."

Leanne walked into the centre of the chamber and looked up. "We've come for our friend!"

"IS THAT SO?" the Spider said. "AND HOW DO YOU EXPECT TO FIND THE OLD MAN?"

"I'll find a way," she said, her voice faltering only a little. "Even if I have to destroy *you* to do it!"

The Spider gave a soft chuckle that made Leanne's flesh crawl. "BEWARE CHILD, THE COLLECTOR MAY FEAR YOU BUT *I* DO NOT! I AM NOT AS EASILY DEFEATED AS THE DRAGON!"

There was an odd humming sound as the insect's dozen eyes considered Leanne. "WHY DON'T WE PLAY A LITTLE GAME? IF YOU MANAGE TO FIND YOUR FRIEND, I'LL LET YOU ALL GO FREE."

"And if we don't?" asked Leanne.

"THEN YOU'LL STAY HERE WITH ME FOR A VERY, VERY LONG TIME!" The Spider laughed sickeningly.

Leanne looked at Hamid, who shook his head and hissed, "It's a trap!"

She shrugged back at him, remembering Jing Shi's warnings. Of course it was all a trap… but what choice did they have?

"We'll play!" she shouted.

The eyes of the Spider sparkled with glee. "EXCELLENT! There was a creak as a heavy door on the far side of the room swung open. "THE CLOCK IS TICKING."

"The pocket watch!" whispered Hamid, reminded by the words of the Spider. He checked the watch. "It's 2:30 am in our time! Less than four hours until the Shang Tower is blown up!"

Leanne looked up again. "How do we know you'll hand Sol over when we find him?"

The Spider snapped, "I ALWAYS KEEP MY WORD... JUST ASK MY CHILDREN!"

The sound of hundreds of armoured feet on stone rose from above. Hamid gasped as a black wave spread down the curved walls from the window above.

"M-more spiders!" he choked.

The Spider demon's children were each the size of a man's hand. And there were thousands of them.

Leanne grabbed Hamid and pulled him towards the door as the wave hit the ground and surged towards them. They slammed it shut just in time.

"They're eating their way through!" cried Hamid as a frantic scratching began on the other side.

Backing away, Leanne took stock of their surroundings. They were in a long corridor with many closed doors leading off. Each door was identical to those in the Shang Tower and bore an apartment number, though the walls looked to be made of ancient stone. Here and there moving residents of the tower flickered in the corridor, as if part of another world…. *Or more likely a different dimension*, thought Leanne, struggling to take it all in.

"This is insane," muttered Hamid. "Where should we go?"

Behind them the wooden door splintered and the first of the spiders scuttled through. Leanne kicked it back with her foot and opened the nearest door, stepping into….

"No!" screamed Hamid, catching her rucksack just in time and pulling her back. Gasping, Leanne saw that the door had opened onto a hundred-metre drop.

The amused voice of the Spider vibrated through the dungeon. "BE CAREFUL WHICH DOOR YOU CHOOSE. ALL MY CHAMBERS ARE DANGEROUS… MOST ARE DEADLY!"

Hamid tugged on Leanne's arm. "More spiders coming through!"

Leanne saw that the door holding them back had all but fallen apart. The heaving wave was flooding towards them. They started running down the corridor, past randomly numbered doors… 78… 125…

Suddenly a man appeared in the corridor ahead. He looked more solid, more real, than the other figures they'd seen… and there was something familiar about his face.

He pointed to the door labelled 96. Then he too flickered and vanished. With no better option, Leanne yanked open the door.

Once they were safely through, Hamid gasped, "That was the man… the man from the second picture in Sol's apartment."

Leanne nodded, recalling the black and white photograph, the man's eyes staring intently at her. "Whatever happened, we were supposed to find our way here," she said. "Let's just hope he was helping us!"

They found themselves standing inside a well-furnished apartment that looked almost exactly like Sol's. The only difference was that three numbered doors were set into the far wall where the window should have been.

Hamid read the door numbers aloud as he moved across the room. "118… 154… 176… Which one do we choose?"

"Watch out!" Leanne cried, lurching forward.

Hamid's foot brushed the tripwire that was strung between the sofas. THUNK! A circular blade the size of a dinner table swooped down from the ceiling....

Leanne collided with Hamid and they crashed to the floor as the blade passed within a whisker. It shot upwards and fell back again in a decreasing arc.

"Remember, every room is a trap!" said Leanne, pulling Hamid to his feet. "The Spider told us so."

Hamid nodded, shakily. "Sorry," he mumbled.

Leanne studied the numbers on the doors. The words of Jing Shi came back to her... '*The answer is in the demon's legs!*'

"You're good at maths, Hamid," she said. "Which of those numbers is a multiple of 8?"

Hamid pointed to the door on the left. "176."

"That's our door," said Leanne, leading the way through into an almost identical apartment. This time they saw two tripwires and avoided them. Three more doors stood before them... 264... 326... 222....

"264!" exclaimed Hamid after some mental calculation. They passed into another room, avoiding a rug in the middle that covered a pit of spikes.

"Why 8?" asked Hamid as they chose a door numbered 488.

Leanne grinned at him. "How many legs does a spider have?"

They followed through more doors… 568… 648… 736….

"Uh-oh," said Hamid as they reached a circular room with twelve doors… and no numbers. Each door bore the image of a different animal…. A tiger…. A dog…. A rabbit….

The gloating voice of the Spider rang out. "YOU HAVE DONE WELL TO GET SO FAR… BUT ONLY ONE DOOR LEADS TO YOUR FRIEND."

Hamid looked at Leanne. "12 in 1 odds of guessing the right door!"

Leanne grinned and gave him a wink. "I don't need to guess."

She approached one of the doors and placed her hand on the handle. She looked back at Hamid and said, "The twelve animals are from the Chinese zodiac. I saw it in Jing Shi's apartment. And the eighth animal is the Goat…."

Holding her breath, she turned the handle and stepped through into a much larger area. The Spider was there, its massive bulk perched atop a spiderweb that stretched across the entire chamber. Wrapped inside a cocoon of green spider silk, Sol dangled from the ceiling amidst hundreds of other objects… swords… shields… and the armour of warriors Leanne assumed had faced the Spider and failed….

"WELL, WELL!" screeched the Spider as it saw her enter. "YOU *HAVE* EXCEEDED MY EXPECTATIONS!"

Leanne smiled at the demon triumphantly. "We passed your test! Now give us Sol!"

The many eyes of the Spider glared at her with malice, but it slashed a strand of silk holding the cocoon. Sol crashed to the ground.

"TAKE HIM," the Spider said.

Leanne stepped forward, but Hamid pulled her back. "Wait," he urged. "To get to Sol, we have to pass right under the Spider." He pointed up at the monstrous creature overhead.

"But we need Sol's help to get out of this," hissed Leanne.

They watched as Sol rolled onto his side, desperation in his eyes. He stared intently on the far side of the room as if signalling to something. In the corner, Leanne saw that the portal key was dangling from a thread high above their heads. To Hamid's left, she spotted a shield hanging low enough for him to reach.

"WHAT ARE YOU WAITING FOR?" the Spider asked, taking a step forward in its web.

Chapter 7

A Narrow Escape

"Look, Hamid, we're going to have to split up," Leanne whispered. "There's no other choice. You go for the key. I'll free Sol! Just remember, only the coils of the spiderweb are sticky. Try to avoid those!"

With a determined nod, Hamid made towards the dangling portal key. As the Spider's piercing eyes followed him, Leanne started advancing to where Sol lay, still bound and struggling on the floor of the chamber. But the Spider had anticipated this. With a scuttling of its clawed feet, the arachnid spun on its web and started towards her.

"NOW YOU'RE BOTH MINE!" it hissed.

Not if I can help it! thought Leanne, the massive bulk looming menacingly above her. She put on a burst of speed and rolled as the Spider lurched forwards. The demon let out a screech of frustration. With her path to Sol blocked, Leanne cast about for another plan of action. Seeing no other way to free her friend, she jumped onto the web and deftly started climbing the thick strands towards the weapons hanging overhead.

The Spider laughed gleefully as the web began to shake. Leanne glanced sideways to see the demon hammering on the threads she was clinging to. Unable to keep her balance she fell, hitting the ground with a thud and landing painfully on her left arm.

"Leanne!" cried Hamid from the other side of the room. "Are you OK?"

"Yes, just about," replied Leanne getting to her feet and flexing her arm to check nothing was broken. Meanwhile, thinking her badly wounded, the Spider had turned its attentions to Hamid. Scuttling forward it began shaking the spiderweb strands beneath his feet.

"Hold on!" shouted Leanne. "And keep moving." With that, she leaped back onto the web, forcing her injured arm to pull her upwards. Torn between its two potential victims, the Spider finally turned and hurried back towards her.

Leanne grabbed the edge of a bronze shield dangling above her head, yanking it down hard. As it came free of the sticky material, she spun and brought it up….

CLANG!

One of the Spider's razor-clawed legs glanced off the shield, knocking Leanne back onto the web. She tried in vain to free herself, her body sticking to the tacky strands.

"DON'T YOU KNOW HOW SPIDERWEBS WORK, LITTLE FLY?" hissed the demon, gleefully. "THE MORE YOU STRUGGLE, THE MORE TRAPPED YOU BECOME!"

'We'll see about that!' cried Leanne. With a burst of strength she pulled herself back onto her feet, ripping the silky strands that held her down.

The Spider let out an angry yell of frustration and shot out another leg towards her. Keeping her balance, Leanne swung the shield to meet her attacker.

CLANG!

This time the Spider was unbalanced as the shield connected. Seeing her chance, Leanne clambered on to another silken web strand. The jewelled hilt of a sword hung just out of reach above her head.

Taking a breath, she jumped and grabbed the sword handle....

For a terrifying moment, Leanne dangled from the sword as it held fast. Then, as the Spider prepared to pounce on her, the sword slid free. Leanne dropped through the web, landing deftly on the stone floor as the Spider flew past.

Seeing that Sol was still some distance from her, Leanne looked about desperately for a way to stop the demon. She saw that four thick, sickly green strands suspended the web from each corner of the room. An idea began to form in her mind.

She ran for the first supporting strand and slashed it with the sword. The entire web shook. On the other side of the chamber, she was relieved to see that Hamid had moved off the web and was now scaling the stone wall. He had already neared the high point where the portal key dangled from the ceiling. Above her, the Spider followed her gaze.

"THE KEY!" it boomed. "THAT'S WHAT YOU WANT IS IT? WELL, THAT KEY IS MINE… AND SO ARE YOU!"

"Hamid, watch out!" cried Leanne as the Spider lurched in his direction.

An armoured foot swiped out at his leg, but Hamid was just out of reach. It struck the wall below his feet, gouging a great lump from the stone. Hamid cried out, almost losing his grip. Leanne raced forward, slashing the second of the supporting strands. The Spider's head jerked round at her.

"WHAT ARE YOU DOING?" it snarled.

Hurrying past Sol, Leanne reached the third support and sliced it in two with the sword. She danced back as the Spider flipped underneath the web and crawled towards her.

"MY BEAUTIFUL WEB!" it screamed, frantically trying to repair the nearest broken support with silk from its abdomen. The entire web was sagging now. Leanne backed towards the final thick strand and raised the sword high.

"This is for Sol," she said.

The Spider's dozen eyes widened as it saw what she was about to do.

"NOOOOOOOOO!"

Leanne swiped the blade through the strand. The web came crashing down, the weight pinning its maker to the ground.

On the other side of the chamber, Hamid gave an elated whoop. He snatched the portal key and climbed hurriedly back down to the ground as Leanne approached the writhing body of the Spider. Its legs were tangled within the silk and it was desperately trying to cut free with its massive mandibles.

"Remember," said Leanne with a mocking tone, "the more you struggle, the more trapped you become!"

The Spider cringed as Leanne held the sword aloft.

"PLEASE!" it whined. "SPARE ME! I WILL HELP YOU DEFEAT THE NEXT DEMON!"

Leanne looked at Hamid. "No way," he said. "We can't trust this monster!"

Leanne nodded in response, but wondered….

"Watch out!" shouted Hamid.

The Spider had cut a leg free and was aiming for Leanne's head! She ducked, rolled and brought the sword down fast. As the blade pierced the demon's body it, and its web, crumbled into a dust that blew across the chamber.

"The Amulet of Shang!" cried Hamid, stepping forward and retrieving another stone piece from the dust. He handed it to Leanne, who pulled the first piece from her pocket. They slotted together perfectly, forming two-thirds of a circle.

Leanne grinned at him. "We did it!"

On the other side of the room, Sol rose stiffly to his feet. The thick green silk that had bound him had also disappeared. "Once again, you've shown great bravery, Leanne," he said, smiling at her. "You really are a marvel."

Leanne felt a blush rising in her cheeks, so she turned away. "How long do we have until the tower is destroyed?" she asked Hamid.

Hamid looked at the pocket watch. "It's 4 am!" he exclaimed. "Just two hours to go!"

Leanne shook her head as she took the portal key from him. "And we don't even know where the next demon is!"

"Yes we do," said Hamid. "Sol have you still got those three pictures you showed us back in your flat?"

"Yes," said Sol, pulling three crumpled photographs from his inside jacket pocket.

"I thought it would be best to remove them from their frames," he explained.

"Great," said Hamid, taking the pictures from Sol and placing them on the floor. "The first photo led us to Jing Shi's apartment, and then we saw this guy in the corridor here," he said, pointing to the staring man.

"You did?" asked Sol, sounding surprised.

"Yes," said Leanne, "or at least some version of him. He helped us to find you."

"Well, well," said Sol shaking his head.

"So," continued Hamid. "There's only one place left to go…."

Chapter 8

Lair of the Serpent

The three friends studied the family portrait – the mother, father and two boys. Then Leanne turned, considering the sword and shield. They'd been decisive in the battle, and she had a feeling they would help out again, even if they were a bit medieval. She slid the sword through her belt and grabbed the shield, holding out the portal key with her other hand.

As before, the picture expanded to envelop her. There was the now familiar lightshow as she was pulled down into a tunnel, closely followed by Hamid and Sol. Then it was over, and they stumbled forward into a new time and place.

They were standing in a brightly decorated flat. Family photographs hung on the walls, flowery curtains covered the windows and colourful cushions were scattered across the comfy-looking sofas.

In the centre of the room stood a man, woman and twin boys. In contrast to the vibrant surroundings, they were ghostly in appearance, their faces drawn and pained.

"The family from the picture," whispered Hamid.

The twin boys stepped forward, arms outstretched. Instinctively Leanne reached out to touch one of them, but her fingers passed right through his ghostly hand.

"The creature you seek dwells on the roof of the tower," said the boy, his voice so faint it seemed to be a whisper of wind.

"Please set us free!" breathed his twin.

With that, their image faded and disappeared. Leanne looked up and saw that the parents had gone as well. *I'll free you all*, she thought resolutely, wondering how many innocent people had been trapped by the Collector and his demons over the years.

"Looks like we're going up," said Hamid, heading out of the flat and down the corridor towards the lift. Unlike the 1950s tower, this version was grimy, with peeling paint on the apartment doors and mould on the walls.

A sign announced that the lift was out of order. "Typical," muttered Sol.

"The stairs it is," said Leanne, pushing open the stairwell door.

"Great," said Hamid, grimacing as he remembered the last time that he and Leanne had climbed the stairs in the Shang Tower. Only a few hours earlier, it now seemed like days ago.

Leanne spotted the first Shade five floors up – a dark shape lurking in the corner of the stairwell. Holding her breath, she motioned for the others to stop and eventually the Shade moved on, unaware of their presence.

Keeping as quiet as possible they encountered several more Shades as they ascended the tower, managing to avoid detection each time. It felt as if the shadowy figures were waiting for something... and Leanne couldn't help wondering if that 'something' was *her*.

Finally they reached the top floor and Leanne peered through the window in the stairwell door to see six Shades roaming the corridor beyond. Halfway along she spotted the emergency exit that led onto the roof.

"The Shades are converging," whispered Sol joining her at the window. "A sign that the evil is getting stronger."

"How do we get past them?" asked Leanne.

"*We* don't," said Hamid, reaching inside his pocket and removing his phone. He turned on the torch app, shining the bright light at Leanne and Sol. "I'm betting this will work almost as well as fire. Give your phone to Sol, Leanne, and we'll hold them off while you go for the roof."

Leanne was about to protest, but Sol placed a restraining hand on her shoulder. "Hamid is right. It's most important that you make it. We'll clear your path."

Seeing the sense of the plan, she nodded, handing her phone to Sol. "Just be careful," she whispered as she prepared to move. "Both of you."

"You look after yourself too," said Hamid, as Sol turned on his torch.

Without another word, Leanne burst through the stairwell door and into the corridor. The Shades screeched and moved to intercept her, but Hamid and Sol hurried behind her, phones raised.

"Back!" yelled Hamid as a Shade cringed away from the bright torch beam.

Leanne pushed the bar to open the emergency exit and took a quick look back. She smiled a little. Her friend's plan was working! The Shades were being held at bay.

Not wasting another second, she hurried out onto a fire escape with ladders leading both up and down the side of the tower. She paused, surprised to see that it was nighttime, the faint light of the moon shining through thin cloud. Without thinking, she looked down and her stomach lurched. The ground was a long way below.

Out of the corner of her eye she noticed a movement – a Shade was rushing at her, fingers outstretched. She dodged and leaped onto the upwards ladder, pulling her focus back to her goal.

She had almost reached the roof... but the Shades were waiting for her. Eight of them formed a hissing circle around the top of the ladder. Spindly shadow hands stretched out for her. Leanne withdrew the sword from her belt, although she knew the steel would probably be useless against these shadow monsters. The nearest Shade rushed forward....

"STOP!" boomed a voice from above. "SHE'S MINE!"

The Shades cowered away at the command.

"ASCEND!" the voice boomed again, and Leanne realized that this time it was speaking to her. Slowly she climbed the final steps to the roof.

A fierce cross-wind blasted her as she stepped onto the top of the Shang Tower. The sky above glittered with stars.

TSSSSSSSSSSSSSS

Leanne gasped at the rasping, reptilian sound. That was no ordinary snake's hiss! The volume suggested something immense! The moon appeared behind a cloud and in the silvery light she saw it….

The Serpent's sleek body was as wide as a car and twenty metres long. Its green and red scales glistened in the moonlight as it uncoiled on the far side of the roof and glided silently towards her. Its head was raised and opened like a hooded cobra, revealing sharp cruel eyes and a mouth with two gleaming white fangs.

"THE COLLECTOR WARNED ME OF YOUR COMING," it hissed, a purple forked tongue flicking in and out as it spoke. "BUT YOU DON'T LOOK DANGEROUSSSS TO ME."

As Leanne held its gaze, she felt her legs weakening and she remembered how a snake could mesmerize its prey. *Look away!* her mind screamed.

With great effort, she wrenched her eyes from the Serpent's. "That's what the Dragon and the Spider thought," she said, trying to sound brave. "And now they're… now they're gone."

The Serpent's forked tongue flickered in a gesture of annoyance. "YOU COMPARE ME TO THOSE LESSER DEMONS?" it said. "LET ME SHOW YOU THE POWER OF THE SSSSSERPENT!"

Its body whipped forward like an uncoiled spring. Leanne barely had time to raise the shield as its mouth opened.

SNAP! Those deadly jaws closed like a mousetrap.

One of the curved fangs had pierced the metal of the shield just above her arm. The Serpent twisted its head, wrenching the shield out of Leanne's hands. As it sailed across the top of the tower, she backed away with the sword raised, ready for the next attack.

"THAT PUNY BLADE CAN'T HURT ME!" the Serpent sneered.

The demon started moving in a wide circle around her. Too late Leanne realized its plan…. The giant snake was surrounding her with its body! With a deadly hiss, it tightened the circle. Leanne gave a cry as the huge coils wrapped around her, pinning one of her arms.

The hooded head of the Serpent rose above Leanne as it began to squeeze the breath from her body.

"MY EMBRACE IS DEADLY!" it gloated, baring its fangs ready to strike. "AND SO IS MY KISSSSS!"

Gasping for air, Leanne flailed uselessly with the sword, but the blade bounced off the thick scales. As her vision began to swim from lack of breath, she cried out for help….

Chapter 9

A Deadly Embrace

"AIIEEEEE!!!"

Leanne was at the very point of blacking out from the Serpent's deadly embrace when the terrible screech filled the air. A shadow fell across her face and she saw the silhouetted fingers of a Shade stretching down towards her… and then reaching instead for the scaly flesh of the reptile! The monster let out a roar of pain as the Shade's hands clawed at its body.

Leanne gasped for breath as the demon released its hold on her. She staggered to her feet, barely keeping her grip on the sword. She watched as two more Shades swept in, screaming and slashing at the writhing demon.

"YOU DARE ATTACK ME?" the Serpent bellowed, thrashing its tail through one of the Shades, obliterating it completely. It opened its jaws and closed them around another of the ghostly shadows, but now more were rushing across the roof from below. "WE SERVE THE SAME MASTER!" boomed the demon.

Leanne looked on in amazement as the Shades continued their attack. None of them seemed to have even noticed she was there.

Hamid ran onto the roof, his face glistening with sweat from the battle below.

"The Shades had us surrounded," Hamid explained breathlessly. "Then you cried out and they flew up here!"

"But why?" said Leanne. "And where's Sol?"

Hamid shook his head as another Shade was destroyed by the Serpent. "We got separated." His voice faltered. "I… I think the Shades got him!"

Leanne was seized by the urge to run down the building to rescue Sol, but she knew what he would say: *defeating the demon is more important.*

She turned her attention back to the ongoing battle. Despite the Shades' superior numbers, the super-powered Serpent clearly had the upper hand, picking the shadowy ghosts off one by one. But this had come at a price – there was no doubt that the demon was weakened… and distracted. Leanne saw her chance.

With a cry, she sprinted forward with the sword raised high…. Aiming for an exposed spot on the Serpent's body….

"NOT SO FASSSST!" it hissed, bringing its massive head round at the very last minute and slamming Leanne hard. She hurtled back across the roof. The sword flew from her grasp and skittered away.

"NOW YOU'RE MINE!" gloated the Serpent, rising above her and slashing apart the remaining Shades with a casual flick of its tail. "THESE LESSSSSER SPIRITSSSS HAVE MERELY POSTPONED YOUR DESSSSTRUCTION!"

Leanne crawled back as the head of the demon arched above her. Its jaws opened, exposing two gleaming fangs ready to strike….

"Leanne!" Hamid's voice cried. "Catch!"

From the corner of her eye, she saw her friend pick up her fallen sword and heave it in her direction. The blade glittered in the air as the Serpent struck.

Leanne reached for the sword as she rolled under the descending fangs…. Her hand closed around the handle and she brought the weapon round, plunging it into the demon….

"AAAARRRGH!" screamed the Serpent as the sword struck deep. Its entire body went rigid. A cracking sound split the air and the giant snake's body split down the middle, crumbling into dust as the two pieces fell away. The demon was defeated!

"Unbelievable!" cried Hamid, running to help Leanne up. "You took that snake down!"

Leanne grinned at him. "*We* took it down."

Hamid reached into the pile of dust and picked out an object. "The last piece of the

Amulet of Shang!" he said triumphantly, holding it up for Leanne to see.

She reached into her backpack to retrieve the other two thirds, but froze as she became aware of more Shades approaching across the roof. They stopped a few metres away, spreading out to block their escape back into the tower.

Hamid looked at Leanne questioningly. "They're not attacking. What are they waiting for?"

"They saved me from the Serpent," she said, still tensed for an attack at any second. "Perhaps they're on our side now."

There was movement on the other side of the roof and the Shades twisted their heads in the direction. A dark figure stepped off the fire escape ladder onto the roof. Leanne almost cried out with relief when she saw who it was.

"Sol!" she called. "You're alive!"

But as the old man raised his head, Leanne realized that something was terribly wrong…. His eyes were shining with a dark red light that seemed to pierce her soul.

Chapter 10

The Collector Revealed

"THANK YOU FOR DESTROYING THE DEMONS," said Sol, his voice booming like those of the evil creatures themselves. "I KNEW I WAS RIGHT... THAT YOU WOULD BE THE ONE TO DESTROY THEM... WITH A LITTLE HELP FROM MY SHADES, OF COURSE."

"Your Shades?" asked Leanne.

"YES, SADLY THE TIME HAS COME TO REVEAL MY TRUE SELF," said Sol. "I HAVE FOUGHT AGAINST THE EVIL FOR SOME SIXTY YEARS, BUT... IN ORDER TO SAVE YOU JUST NOW, LEANNE... I HAD TO GIVE IN."

"Give in to what?" said Leanne, confused.

"TO THE EVIL THAT I UNLEASHED," sighed Sol. "FOR YOU SEE… I WAS THE ONE WHO STARTED ALL THIS!"

"He's…" Hamid began, his voice breaking. "*He's… the Collector….* Leanne, it was him all along!"

Leanne shook her head in disbelief. Could it be that through all their adventures the Collector had been the one guiding them? *No, it couldn't be Sol!*

But the words of Jing Shi came back to her: *the power of the demons corrupts all who come into contact with them.*

"I'M AFRAID HAMID'S RIGHT," boomed Sol. "I TOOK THE URN FROM ITS RESTING PLACE IN CHINA… I RELEASED ITS POWER HERE IN THE SHANG TOWER."

"But why?" gasped Leanne, filled with a terrible sense of desperation. If Sol could be corrupted by the evil, what hope did she have of defeating it?

"I DIDN'T MEAN TO, NOT THAT IT MATTERS NOW…" the old man paused. "THE AMULET OF SHANG," he said, stretching out his hand as he approached. The Shades backed away submissively, clearly under his control. "GIVE IT TO ME."

Leanne fitted the final piece of the amulet together. The stone circle glowed blue in her hands and she felt a surge of energy run through her body. She looked at Sol, who gave her a sly smile, his eyes manic and power-hungry, completely unlike those of the man she knew.

Leanne backed away, holding the amulet in front of her. "You have to fight this, Sol!"

"THE HUMAN YOU CALL SOL WILL SOON BE NO MORE," he rasped, seeming to grow in size as he approached. "THERE WILL ONLY BE… THE COLLECTOR!"

He threw his arms wide and a blast of air swept across the roof, driving Leanne and Hamid to the very edge of the building. Even the Shades cowered away from it.

Hamid looked at the forty-storey drop to the ground and then at Leanne. "We can't let him have the amulet!"

"I don't intend to," replied Leanne, removing the portal key from her pocket.

"GIVE ME THE AMULET OR I'LL BE FORCED TO SET MY SHADES ON YOU," threatened the Collector.

Leanne saw the ghostly shadows closing in on them now, blocking any escape route back across the roof. She looked over the side of the building.

"Perhaps we could just jump!" Hamid cried.

Concentrating hard, Leanne waved the key over the side of the building. A swirling portal formed just a couple of metres below them. She grabbed Hamid's arm....

"I was joking!" he protested as she pulled him over the edge.

Leanne and Hamid fell through space.... Into the portal and through the time stream. Seconds later, they were thrown out the other side.

They tumbled across a smooth hard floor, coming to rest in a heap.

"We're back in the 1950s, in the lobby of the Shang Tower!" exclaimed Hamid, seeing the polished floor and the bright clean walls. He pulled out the pocket watch. "And it's 5:52 am! We've got less than ten minutes until this place is blown up in our time!"

There was a screech from the direction of the portal, which hovered a few metres away. The spindly fingers of a Shade appeared through the spinning vortex.

"Come on!" she exclaimed as she pushed herself up, trying to ignore the exhaustion from her latest battle. "We have to find the urn and put an end to all this!"

She bolted towards the stairs leading down to the basement, the screaming of the Shades echoing across the lobby.

"Slow down!" said Hamid as they took the stairs two at a time. "Shouldn't we be searching Sol's apartment? The urn has to be there!"

"No," replied Leanne, scanning the basement. "Sol wouldn't be that stupid. This is the perfect place to hide it."

Leanne started searching the basement. "It *has* to be here. Ground zero at 6 am. The perfect place to destroy…" She stopped short as she saw an object covered in a tarpaulin right next to one of the columns. She pulled the cover away sharply. "The urn!"

A metre high, the urn was made of a dull green stone and covered in intricate Chinese carvings. The Dragon was depicted there. And the Spider and Serpent. *Time to seal you up for good*, thought Leanne as she removed the Amulet of Shang from her backpack.

"Now how do I use this thing?" she wondered aloud.

"EXCELLENT QUESTION," the booming voice of the Collector made the walls of the basement vibrate. "AND ONE I HAVE NO INTENTION OF ANSWERING. GIVE ME THE AMULET!"

"I'll keep him busy while you work out what to do!" Hamid said to Leanne.

Before she could stop him, Hamid threw himself at the Collector. But the frail form of the old man now possessed an inhuman strength. He grabbed Hamid, lifted him clean off the floor and then threw him across the basement. Hamid landed with a thud against one of the columns.

"THREE MINUTES UNTIL THIS BUILDING IS DESTROYED AND THE URN WITH IT!" The Collector gloated, blocking Leanne's way to help Hamid. "THEN I WILL BE FREE TO ENSLAVE THE WORLD WITH MY SHADES!"

"I still don't understand," Leanne said, playing for time. "Why did you help us to destroy the demons."

"WITH YOUR HELP, I THOUGHT I COULD FIGHT THE EVIL INSIDE ME!" The Collector's face twisted into an evil smile, so unlike Sol. "BUT I WAS WRONG! NOW I

AM STRONGER THAN I HAVE EVER BEEN… AND WITH THE AMULET… WHICH NOW CONTAINS THE POWER OF ALL THREE DEMONS… I'LL BE INVINCIBLE!"

The Collector's hand shot out and closed around Leanne's throat, squeezing like a steel trap. She gasped for breath as he lifted her off her feet. Her vision swam as she looked into those blazing red eyes…. And for a moment she thought she heard the Sol she knew, whispering to her….

"Destroy the amulet!"

Leanne held the Amulet of Shang up in her hands. The Collector's blazing eyes widened. And she threw it down with all her might….

The amulet smashed into a thousand pieces, casting a wave of energy as it did so. A massive crack formed, splitting the floor of the basement in two.

Leanne fell to the ground beside the crack, turning to see the urn tumble into it. It fell into the depths of the earth, flames rising up to engulf it.

Beside her, bathed in the released energy from the amulet the Collector had crashed to the ground and now lay still.

Leanne rose slowly, relieved to see that Hamid was getting to his feet on the other side of the basement. She moved towards the fallen body of the Collector…. His eyes were no longer glowing and she sensed that the evil had been driven out of Sol. She knelt at his side and he looked at her with vague recognition.

"Sol!" she sobbed. "I didn't mean to hurt you!"

"You saved me!" he said, his voice almost too weak to hear. "Now get out of here! Use the key to escape."

Hamid tapped her urgently on the shoulder, shoving the pocket watch in front of her eyes. "This place is about to blow in 10… 9… 8!"

Leanne rose and waved the portal key before her one last time. The glowing circle of light appeared.

"6… 5… 4…"

Leanne took Hamid's hand and pulled him through the portal…

…into daylight. A cool breeze touched Leanne's cheeks and she realized they were standing outside, some distance from the Shang Tower. A number of other people were crowded nearby behind a yellow safety barrier, wrapped up against the morning air.

"3… 2… 1…"

Leanne looked at the Shang Tower, stark against the dawn sky, one last time.

BOOM!

Despite the incredible noise of the explosion and the smoke rising from the base, the tower stood motionless for a moment. Then its structure seemed to crumple all at once, walls and balconies collapsing straight down. Only as the top floors fell did it start to list, crashing to the right and sending a thick cloud across the open ground. The dust reminded Leanne of the remains of the demons they'd battled over the course of that night… as the tower and its darkness fell into rubble forever.

"I can't believe it's gone," Hamid said at her side.

Leanne looked up at the clear morning sky. No demons. No Shades. She allowed herself a smile. "It's finally over," she said.

As the ruin of the Shang Tower settled, the assembled spectators began to move away. Leanne found she recognized many of the faces as former residents of the tower! There was the man from the Spider's dungeon, smartly dressed and with his arm around a woman. The family from the colourful apartment was there, the parents now lined and grey and beside them the twins, more than twice her own age.

She spotted other faces from the photographs in Sol's apartment… except now they were smiling. In fact, there was almost a party atmosphere, as if the crowd realized that the destruction of the Shang Tower was a cause for celebration.

"Jing Shi!" gasped Hamid.

Leanne turned and saw the little Chinese woman approaching through the dispersing throng. Amazingly, she didn't look a day older than when they had met her over sixty years earlier… and she was elderly then.

"You have triumphed over the evil of the Collector," she said, smiling warmly. "Just as I knew you would."

"How… how are you here?" Leanne asked.

Jing Shi shrugged. "I have my ways. And I could not resist being here to see the tower destroyed… and to congratulate you both. Look around…" She indicated the familiar faces in the crowd. "Your defeat of the Collector has changed the timeline. These people had another chance at life… a happier life without darkness."

Leanne shook her head in disbelief, but was struck by a sudden thought. "What about Sol?"

Jing Shi touched her arm and nodded towards the yellow barrier. A slender-framed man was standing there, wispy white hair blowing in the breeze, his tweed jacket pulled tightly around him. Leanne's heart leaped as she recognized Sol.

Leanne turned back to ask the old woman a question, but she had disappeared.

Then the old man Leanne had called her friend approached. "Excuse me," said Sol's familiar voice. "But have we… met somewhere before?"

Leanne smiled up at him. "No… I don't think so," she said. "Did you live here in the Shang Tower?"

"I believe so," he said with a frown. "But my memory isn't what it used to be." His eyes widened with interest. "My goodness! That's quite an interesting artefact you have there!"

It took a second for Leanne to realize he was referring to the portal key, which was still clenched in her hand. She held it out so he could take a better look.

"Sixteenth-century Chinese, I'd say," murmured Sol, turning it over in his hands. "Could be worth a pretty penny. Wherever did you get it?"

Leanne and Hamid exchanged amused glances.

"A collector gave it to us," they said.

THE END

FICTION EXPRESS

THE READERS TAKE CONTROL!

Have you ever wanted to change the course of a plot, change a character's destiny, tell an author what to write next?

Well, now you can!

'Ghost Tower' was originally written for the award-winning interactive e-book website Fiction Express.

Fiction Express e-books are published in gripping weekly episodes. At the end of each episode, readers are given voting options to decide where the plot goes next. They vote online and the winning vote is then conveyed to the author who writes the next episode, in real time, according to the readers' most popular choice.

www.fictionexpress.co.uk

WINNER
Education Resources
Award for Innovation

FICTION EXPRESS

TALK TO THE AUTHORS

The Fiction Express website features a blog where readers can interact with the authors while they are writing. An exciting and unique opportunity!

FANTASTIC TEACHER RESOURCES

Each weekly Fiction Express episode comes with a PDF of teacher resources packed with ideas to extend the text.

"The teaching resources are fab and easily fill a whole week of literacy lessons!"
Rachel Humphries, teacher at Westacre Middle School

Clock
by Andrew G Taylor

Harry Boyd can stop time – literally. This enables him to live a life of petty crime under the very noses of other shoppers at the Gatesworth Shopping Centre. Then one day, he is surprisingly caught in the act, and everything starts to unravel....

Will Harry and his fellow clock-stoppers succeed in preventing the disaster threatening planet Earth?

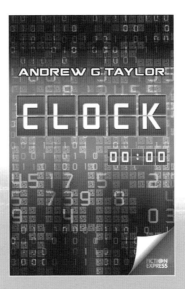

ISBN 978-1-78322-555-2

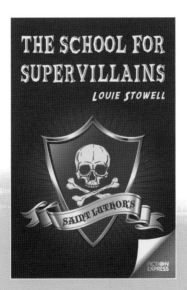

FICTI●N EXPRESS

Mind Swap
by Alex Woolf

Simon Archer is a bully. He's nasty to his classmates, his teachers, his mum. Then, one morning, Simon looks in the mirror and gets a shock. The face staring back at him is not his own. Who did this to him? And will anyone ever believe who he really is?

Simon's body has changed – but can he ever change inside?

ISBN 978-1-78322-550-7

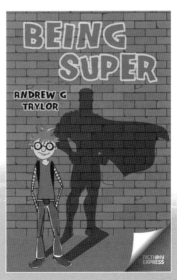

About the Author

Andrew G Taylor was born in New Zealand, grew up in England and now lives in Australia. He's the writer of the 'Superhumans' series and The Adjusters. His work has been shortlisted for the Waterstones Children's Book Award and the Northern Ireland Book Award.

A former teacher who has lived around the world, Andrew uses the places he has visited and the many computer games he's played as inspiration for his writing.